The
MYSTERIOUS MAKERS
of Shaker Street

THAT'S
the
SPIRIT!

The Mysterious Makers of Shaker Street
is published by Stone Arch Books,
A Capstone Imprint
1710 Roe Crest Drive
North Mankato, Minnesota 56003
www.mycapstone.com

Cataloging-in-Publication Data is available on the
Library of Congress website.

ISBN: 978-1-4965-4678-4 (library binding)
ISBN: 978-1-4965-4682-1 (paperback)
ISBN: 978-1-4965-4686-9 (eBook PDF)

Summary: The Mysterious Makers work together
to prove to their friend's house is not haunted.

Design Elements: Shutterstock: Master3D, PremiumVector

Designer: Tracy McCabe

Printed in Canada.
010382F17

The
MYSTERIOUS MAKERS
of Shaker Street

THAT'S
the
SPIRIT!

by Stacia Deutsch

illustrated by Robin Boyden

STONE ARCH BOOKS
a capstone imprint

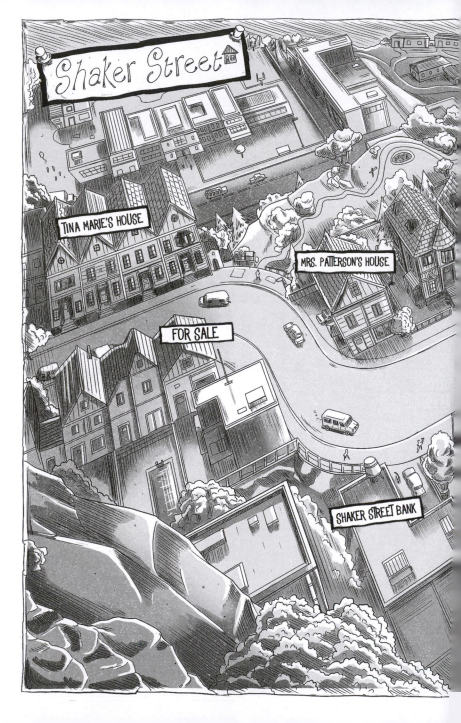

CHAPTER ONE

"Did you hear the news?" Liv Hernandez blurted out. She didn't even say hi first. She walked right up to Michael and Leo and announced, "Tina Maria Carlos is moving away."

Michael Wilson and Leo Hammer were sitting on Michael's front porch steps, working on Leo's computer.

Leo had been having trouble with the cooling fan inside the laptop. It was supposed to blow all the time so the computer wouldn't overheat.

Instead, Leo's fan was starting up with a weird soft humming sound and seconds later, it would sputter and die.

The computer was a present from Michael. He'd rescued it from the trash and fixed it up. Sometimes things didn't work the way they should. Today was one of those days. It was bad for a computer to get too hot. It could even start a fire if they weren't careful.

The two boys were so involved in the problem that for a moment, they didn't understand what Liv was saying. They both stared up at her.

"Tina Maria is MOOOVING," she announced again in a loud, clear voice.

"Huh?" Michael asked. When he was working hard on something, it took a while to get his attention. He tipped back his baseball cap and stared up at his cousin.

Liv and Michael were both ten years old. Like their moms, who were sisters, they were best friends. Their other friend Leo was nine. Leo was so smart, he'd skipped a grade and was in Liv and Michael's class.

As the reality of what Liv said sunk in, Leo jumped up off the steps. "Tina Maria?" he exclaimed. "But she just moved here!"

Leo spent a lot of time with Tina Maria. They were both great at math. Their teacher had picked the two of them to represent the school in a citywide math competition.

"It can't be true," Leo insisted. "Tina Maria didn't tell me she was moving. I just talked to her yesterday. No way." He pushed back his long sandy brown hair to get a good look at Liv's face.

"Yes way," Liv replied.

"Are you sure?" Michael asked Liv. He squinted at her sideways. "Maybe you heard wrong?"

"Tina Maria told me herself," Liv said, shaking her head hard. Her dark brown ponytails swished, and her glasses slipped down her nose. She pushed up her red frames and said, "The moving truck's coming tomorrow."

Leo started down the porch steps. Michael's house was at the top of a long hill on Shaker Street. Tina Maria lived near the bottom.

Leo hated going up and down the hill, but this was important.

"I'm going to talk to her. She can't leave town! The math competition is in two weeks." Leo put his hands on his hips. "I have to convince her to stay."

"How are you going to do that?" Liv asked him.

"I don't know yet. Maybe I'll start with begging." He imitated the way he'd do it. *"Please, don't leave. Please."* Leo looked at Liv and asked, "Do you think it'll work?"

"You need to convince her parents," Liv said. "She's leaving because *they* want to move."

"Hmm." Leo considered the problem. "I think I should bring them a present." He checked his pockets. They were empty.

"I don't have money for flowers or candy," he said. Turning back, he asked Michael, "What can we make?"

Michael set Leo's computer down on the porch. "Let's go see," he said.

Michael's family lived in a tall, purple Victorian house. His grandfather — his dad's dad — lived in a round tower on the top floor. Grandpa's glass windows overlooked the whole street, and all the kids in the neighborhood called him Grandpa Henry.

When Grandpa Henry retired, he'd given his backyard toolshed to Michael and his friends. They used it as a clubhouse. The shelves were stacked with things that Michael had found at garage sales and in neighborhood dumpsters. They called the clubhouse the Maker Shack.

Michael believed that nothing should be thrown away. Anything could be used to make something new.

"Tina Maria likes gardening," Liv said as they went through the gate to the backyard. "I think we should make her family a box to plant seeds in." She reached out for the doorknob to the Maker Shack. "I think there are some recycled wood pieces behind the —"

Michael grabbed her hand.

"Wait!" he said, pulling her fingers off the knob. "Something's wrong."

He pointed at a thin white string. It stretched down from the house's tower window to the top of the Maker Shack door.

"What's that?" Leo asked Michael. "Are you and Grandpa Henry working on a project? Maybe some kind of telephone wire?"

Liv giggled. She was the only one of the three of them who had a cell phone. "Are you talking about an old tin-can phone?" she asked. "The kind where Grandpa Henry would have a can on one end and Michael would have a can on the other?"

"That's actually a good idea," Michael said. "It would stop Grandpa from yelling out the window all the time. Maybe I'll make one later."

Then Michael looked at the string and frowned. "But this isn't for a can phone. So what's it doing here?"

Michael glanced up toward the tower window. Grandpa Henry was standing in the frame. They could all see him smiling. He shouted down at them. "Go on, you whippersnappers. Open the shack!"

"That means we *shouldn't* open it," Leo said, stepping back. "Something bad will happen if we do."

"You always think something bad is about to happen," Liv teased as she reached for the knob. "Leo's a chicken."

"Yep. Bawk-bawk," Leo admitted.

"I agree with Leo," Michael said, squinting at the string. "Don't pull the doorknob, Liv."

Leo could see it now. The cord was attached to something at the top of the door. Grandpa Henry loved to prank them. They never knew what he might do. Or when it would happen. This seemed suspicious. What was he up to this time?

"You two are silly. Nothing will happen," Liv assured them.

She pulled open the door to the Maker Shack. When the wooden door swung open a crack, a little bell rang.

"That's it?" Michael said. "A bell?" He glanced up at his grandfather, who was still watching from the window.

Leo could now see that Grandpa Henry was pulling the string to ring the bell. He smiled and waved.

Leo waved back.

"See? That wasn't so *baaaaa*—" Liv started to say. But when she pushed the door the rest of the way open, a bucket fell from the doorframe.

Hundreds of feathers fell out, covering all three of them with white and yellow fluff. The bell was just a distraction. Grandpa had tricked them!

Leo started to laugh. "You always say I'm a chicken," he told Liv. "But we *all* look like chickens now!"

Liv and Michael laughed.

"Gotcha, whippersnappers!" Grandpa Henry shouted out from the tower window. Then he disappeared from their sight. But his heavy laughter continued to echo through the backyard for a few more moments.

Leo looked around and said, "What a mess!"

They started pulling feathers out of their hair and off their clothes.

"Look on the bright side. We can totally use these feathers for a project," Michael said. He began collecting them in a small bag. The others joined him.

"Maybe we can use them to decorate the flower box for Tina Maria's parents," Leo suggested. He sneezed and three feathers fell off his head. "I hope the present will convince them to stay."

A raspy voice called through the shed. "Nothing will convince them. Mom and Dad refuse to stay here on Shaker Street," the voice said.

Leo, Michael, and Liv all turned to find Tina Maria standing in the doorway. Her black hair was pulled back neatly in a headband. She was wearing a blue T-shirt that said "Wizard in Training" across the front, and she was carrying a small green purse.

"We have to move away," Tina Maria continued sadly.

Leo stood up and hurried over to her. With every step, more feathers fell off him. "It's not fair," he moaned.

"I know!" Tina Maria said. Her voice was tight and cracked. "I don't want to leave Shaker Street."

Liv had somehow gotten all the feathers out of her hair, except the few she left in for decoration. She hurried over to Tina Maria and put her arm around her friend's shoulders. "Why are you moving?" she asked. "And why is it so sudden?"

Tina Maria sighed. She pinched her lips together and whispered, "Our house is haunted."

CHAPTER TWO

"Okay, you should definitely move then," Leo said without hesitation. "I'd move too."

"But I don't want to leave school," Tina Maria told him.

"How about buying a different house on Shaker Street?" Leo asked. "That would be better than living in a haunted house." He shivered and wrapped his arms around himself.

"I like my house," Tina Maria protested.

"There's no reason to move. There's no such thing as a haunted house," Michael said, practical as usual.

He grabbed a few bins off a nearby shelf and set them on the workbench. They had made the bench themselves from an old door that rested on top of two fruit crates.

"Ghosts exist," Liv put in. "I know, because I'm an expert. But we can live happily with them if we try. Have you tried to talk to the ghost? Make friends with it?"

"You can't live happily with a ghost!" Leo protested. "You gotta move away."

"Leo!" Liv said firmly. "Stop it. You're scaring Tina Maria."

"She scared me first," Leo protested. "So we're even."

"There's no such thing as ghosts," Michael said. He was setting things from the bins out on the table. He had a flashlight, batteries, and a compass.

"Where's the Maker Sack?" Michael asked Liv. The sack was an old backpack that Michael had found in the trash at school. Liv had duct taped the holes and written *MAKER SACK* on it in silver tape.

Liv found it by her beanbag chair, which Michael had rescued from a dumpster and fixed up. She gave the sack to him.

"Thanks," Michael said.

While Michael continued to rummage through plastic bins and cardboard boxes, Liv let Tina Maria sit in Leo's chair. It was an old plastic chair that Michael had bought at a garage sale for two dollars.

Leo's computer desk space was made out of an unfinished piece of wood held up by two piles of bricks.

Tina Maria leaned back in the chair. It creaked.

Leo jumped at the sound. Liv and Michael giggled.

"What? I'm nervous!" Leo squeaked.
"Even the thought of ghosts on Shaker Street
frightens me."

Liv shook her head and said to Tina
Maria, "Sorry about Chicken-Boy here."

Leo tucked his hands in his armpits and
bawked again.

Liv went to her neat corner of the shack. She got a small notebook and opened the cover. "So, Tina Maria, tell us about the ghost."

"He . . . ," Tina Maria began.

"He . . . ," Liv wrote that down in her journal. "You know for certain it's a boy?"

"A man," Tina Maria said. "I know for certain that the ghost is General Pablo Carlos. He was my grandfather."

"General Carlos?" Leo was suddenly interested. "That's your grandfather? There's a statue of him in the park," he said. "He was a hero!" He put up a finger. "Wait. Don't say anything else. Hang on."

Leo went running out of the shack to the porch of Michael's house. He grabbed his laptop and came right back.

Leo set the computer on the workbench next to some magnets that Michael had found. He booted it and waited for the screen to light up.

"Blast! I forgot it's not working . . ." He looked over at Liv. "I want to read about General Carlos on the web. Can I use your phone?"

Michael hadn't said much since Tina Maria had arrived. He looked up from his project and said, "Come on, Leo. You know the rules."

"You can't be serious, Michael," Leo complained. "What am I supposed to do? My computer fan's busted."

Michael shrugged and pointed at the large piece of cardboard tacked to the wall. In permanent pen it said:

**The Mysterious Makers
of Shaker Street Promise**

1) We turn old things into new things.

**2) We don't use new things if we can
use old things.**

Leo had scribbled at the bottom:

Computers are okay.

Liv had added:

Phones are okay if zombies attack. Call me!

The last line read:

This contract is legally binding.

"We need new rules," Leo whined, even though he was the one who insisted on the last part about it being legal. His dad was a lawyer, and Leo liked learning about laws.

"Our rules work great," Michael told him. He put the magnets in the Maker Sack and went over to Tina Maria. "Tell us about the first time you saw the ghost."

"At first, I didn't see him," she admitted. "I heard him."

"*Hmm,*" Michael said. He went to a bin on the left side of the room and pulled out a digital thermometer. After putting that in the backpack, he said, "What did the ghost sound like?"

"Regular ghost noises," Tina Maria explained. "*Oooh. Ohhh.*" She imitated what a ghost might sound like in a Halloween haunted house.

Michael looked to Liv with a questioning look. A few weeks earlier, she'd told him that real ghosts didn't sound like they did on TV or in the movies. Liv believed that ghosts made breathy, growling sounds, never "*Oooh. Ohhh.*"

"Are you sure it's a ghost?" Liv asked Tina Maria.

Tina Marie nodded, but Liv kept talking. "Ghosts don't usually sound like that. Is it possible that someone left a TV on? Or it kind of sounds like a fan."

She imitated one going, *"Whir. Whir,"* which did sound a lot like *"Oooh. Ohhh."*

"It's a ghost. I'm positive." Tina Maria went on, "The *ooh* sound was just the first time. The General talks too."

At that, Liv smiled. "What does he say?"

"Stuff like, 'Get out of my house,' and, 'You don't belong here.'" Tina Maria imitated a man's deep, throaty voice. "'Run for your lives!'"

"So, mean and spooky things?" Leo asked. He turned off his computer. It wasn't working anyway.

"He wants us to get out of the house," Tina Maria said. "That's what my aunts and uncle did."

"Your aunts and uncle lived in the house too?" Michael asked, stepping closer to listen to her story.

"My oldest aunt didn't even make it one night," Tina Maria admitted. "She saw a glowing figure in the middle of the night, and that was it. She moved out the next day. My other aunt made it for a whole week before she left."

"How many times have people moved in and out?" Michael asked. He pointed at Liv and her notebook and asked, "Are you writing all this down, Liv?"

"Got it," Liv assured him.

"The General had four children. Aunt Rosa, Uncle Federico, Aunt Julia, and my dad." Tina Maria held up four fingers. "My dad is the youngest. The others all tried to live in the house, but got scared. My dad is the last of the General's kids to try staying there." She added, "I know it's weird, but no one even called him 'Grandpa.' We all called him 'the General.'"

"'The General' sounds scarier," Leo said. Then he asked, "Why would your parents want to live there if everyone else ran away? That doesn't sound very smart to me."

"Because we needed a new house. Shaker Street is the best place to live. My dad thought he wouldn't be scared of his own father. He kept asking 'Why would a ghost scare his own family away?'" Tina Maria sighed. "It doesn't make sense."

"Tina Maria is right," Liv agreed. "You'd think the ghost would want to hang around with his kids and grandkids."

"If there was such a thing as ghosts, I'm sure my grandfather would want to haunt our house forever," Michael joked. "He'd stay up in his room and play tricks on us."

"It would be the same as now," Liv said, smiling. "Nothing would change."

They laughed.

"You've been living there a few months," Leo said. "Has the ghost been around this whole time?"

"No. He didn't show up until last week," Tina Maria said. "My mom heard his voice. After that, she saw a shadow in a mirror. We've seen him and heard him a lot since then."

Leo fearfully clenched his fists. "How do you know it's the General?" he asked.

"When he appears in the mirror, he's always wearing his uniform," Tina Maria told him. "At first, my parents tried not to be afraid. They told the ghost to go away. They told him that we would never move away. But the General didn't care. The other night, he did the scariest thing ever . . ."

CHAPTER THREE

"What did he do?!" Leo moved closer to Michael, as if Michael could protect him from the story.

"The General left a note," Tina Maria said. She reached into her purse and pulled out a small empty glass jar. "It was in here." Tina Maria glanced around at Liv, Michael, and Leo. "I'm hoping you can help get rid of the ghost before we have to leave town."

Michael stepped forward. "We can help," he said confidently. "I know we can."

Liv stepped up next to Michael. "If there *is* a ghost," she said, "we can teach him to live in peace with you and your family." Liv put her hand on Tina Maria's arm and said, "You could bake cookies together."

"It's a bad idea to go looking for a ghost," Leo advised them all. "We're just going to make the General mad. Then, if he wants to attack someone, he'll go for the slow, little guy." He pointed at himself and said, "That's me."

"You'll be okay," Michael assured Leo. He slipped on light blue medical gloves and told Tina Maria, "Let me see what you brought."

Tina Maria handed Michael the jar. It was slender, but tall. The smooth glass was blue but didn't have any designs.

"The jar looks new to me. But the note was on old paper in fancy writing," Tina Maria explained. "When my dad took the note, I snuck the jar away."

"Can I try something?" Michael asked her. "A science experiment?"

"Sure." Tina Maria nodded.

Michael went to a high shelf. He stood on a stool and brought down some baby powder and a small, clean paintbrush. Tina Maria set the jar on the table.

While he poured a light dusting of baby powder on the outside of the jar, he asked her, "What did the note say?"

"Get out. Leave this house and never come back," Tina Maria said.

"*Hmm . . .*" Michael nodded as he brushed off the baby powder with the brush.

Some of the powder stuck to the side of the glass, revealing fingerprints.

From another shelf, Michael got a magnifying glass. He asked Tina Maria, "Who has touched this glass?"

She thought about it a minute and said, "Me and Dad. That's all."

"Your mom never touched it?" Michael asked, turning the jar in his hand.

"No. My dad found it on the kitchen counter," Tina Maria said. "I brought it straight here."

Michael rotated the jar in his hands so the others could see. He said, "Fingerprints are all unique to our fingers. I can tell that there are three different prints on this glass." He pointed them each out, counting, "One. Two. Three."

"Three?" Leo questioned. "You're wearing gloves, so that means the only other one who might have touched the glass is the ghost. Ghosts don't have fingerprints!"

"Exactly!" Michael cheered at the discovery. He swung the Maker Sack over his shoulders and said, "Come on. Let's go to Tina Maria's house. We're going to prove there's no such thing as ghosts."

CHAPTER FOUR

Tina Maria's house was the third house on the right past a curve in the road. It was blue with brown trim. Like most of the houses on Shaker Street, the house was narrow and had three floors. The movers were already there, busy packing boxes.

"Wow," Leo said. "Looks like you're almost ready to leave. Your parents must really be scared."

He looked around. The kitchen was almost all ready to go. There were boxes marked *GLASSES* and *PLATES*.

"Hi," Tina Maria's Aunt Julia greeted the kids. "Did you come to help?" She was stacking bowls onto the counter.

"Sort of," Michael said, patting his Maker Sack.

"We came to meet the ghost," Liv said. "We're going to convince him to let Tina Maria's family stay."

"Oh," Aunt Julia seemed surprised. She lowered her brown eyes and pushed back her dark hair. In a whispered voice she said, "You know about the General?"

"Yes, but I don't believe it," Michael told her quietly.

"You should," she replied. "I was here for a single night. When I saw him, I moved out. I didn't even care if I got to keep the house or not. I wasn't bringing my husband or our pets here." She rubbed her arms and said, "It was terrifying. He *glows*."

"Glows?" Michael asked, pinching his lips together thoughtfully.

Liv held up her notebook and said, "I'm going to write a news article about the ghost. My favorite magazine *Suspicious Surprises* is going to want this story."

Michael rolled his eyes.

"I think your notes will help prove that there's *no* ghost," he told Liv. He turned to Aunt Julia and asked, "You say the General glows? Is he a certain color?"

"Well, the ghost is kind of clear, but the space around him is brown," Aunt Julia said. "It's like he has a muddy shadow. So creepy!"

"Way creepy," Leo said.

"It's normal for ghosts to have shadows. They're called orbs or auras," Liv told her friends. "I read in a book that there are ten different colors of ghostly orbs. White ghosts want to communicate. Green glowing ones are looking for love."

"What about brown shadow ghosts?" Leo asked. The minute he asked, he regretted it. He didn't really want to know the answer.

Liv said, "It's not safe to be around ghosts with brown or black glowing shadows. Those are the evil ones."

"I think I hear my dad calling," Leo said, cupping his ear with his hand. "I gotta go."

Michael grabbed his arm. "There's no ghost," he insisted. "Not one with green or brown or purple shadows. It's ridiculous."

"I know what I saw," Aunt Julia said. "It was definitely a ghost."

Leo didn't like any of this. He wanted to leave, but Michael refused to let go of his arm. Instead, Michael led him into the living room. It was a small room with a brick fireplace. Above the fireplace was a large mirror.

"Is that where everyone sees the General?" Michael asked Tina Maria. The glass was huge. It went from the top of the fireplace all the way to the ceiling. The frame looked antique.

"Yes," Tina Maria said. "He was so big. He filled the entire frame."

"That mirror was here when I was a child," Tina Maria's Uncle Federico said as he came into the room. His large black mustache jiggled. "It was so high, we had to stand on a chair to see ourselves. I've always loved this house. It's not so nice now . . . if you know what I mean." He shivered.

"Did you see the ghost?" Leo asked.

Uncle Federico began taking books off a bookshelf. He flipped through the pages, checking inside each one before he set it into the crate.

"No." He looked over his shoulder and admitted, "I didn't stay long enough in the house." He puffed out his chest. "I wasn't scared but my wife, Angelina, was terrified. She was so scared she couldn't sleep. It was terrible. We had to leave."

Angelina's voice came from upstairs. "Federico, don't tell those children that made-up story! You were the one who wanted to move. When we lived here, you spent the whole time locked in the closet."

"The walls in this house are very thin," Federico said with a grimace.

"And your wife has very good hearing," Angelina called back down the stairs. "I'm packing sheets and towels. How are the books coming along?" she asked.

"Great," Federico shouted back even though there were only three books in the crate. "Some of these belonged to the General. They're old and very valuable," he said and then sighed deeply. "I better get to work. We need to finish this all before the truck comes tomorrow." He piled more boxes into the crate.

"Where are Mom and Dad?" Tina Maria asked.

"They went to buy more boxes," Federico said. "You have a lot of stuff."

Michael looked around the room and thoughtfully said, "Maybe you should sell some things from the house. You could have a garage sale."

Tina Maria was sad. "I don't want a garage sale. I don't want to pack. I don't want to move."

Michael nodded. "Okay. Let's get started on this ghost problem. Where was the last place the ghost appeared?"

"We haven't seen him for a couple days," Tina Maria said. "But last night, I *heard* the General in my bedroom."

CHAPTER FIVE

On the way to her room, Tina Maria pointed at several portraits on the stairs. The first one was a woman. "This is my grandmother, the General's wife. She died before I was born," Tina Maria explained.

She stopped and pointed at the next picture.

"That's him. That's the General," she said. In the large painting was a broad man with a bushy mustache and thin beard.

He was wearing a dark green uniform. On his shoulders were pads with golden fringe. Pinned to his chest were medals and bars with colorful ribbons.

"General Carlos was a hero," Leo said, taking a long look at the painting. "I just don't understand how someone so loved could become . . . ," he dropped his voice to a whisper, ". . . evil."

Liv studied the painting, then suggested, "Maybe he's trying to communicate with his family. He probably has something to say."

"You mean, like maybe he wants to tell us where he put his will?" Tina Maria suggested before heading up the stairs toward her room.

"Wait!" Michael hurried after her, climbing the steps two at a time.

"What did you just say?" Liv asked. "This sounds important."

"Oh." Tina Maria turned back toward them all. She was at the top of the steps. "Didn't I tell you? After the General died, no one could find his will." She glanced up at the man's portrait. "It's somewhere in the house, but no one knows where."

"That's interesting," Liv said, writing a note in her journal. "No will. Fascinating," she muttered.

Since Leo knew the most about laws, he said, "The will probably says who officially owns the house. Without a will, it could belong to anyone."

"That's a problem," Michael said.

"My family decided we didn't need the will," Tina Maria said.

She went on to explain. "At first, we all agreed to give the house to my Aunt Rosa. She's the oldest child, so that made sense. But then she got scared away by the ghost. Uncle Federico and Aunt Angelina took the house next, since Federico is the second child. But they got scared too. Aunt Julia was third. She saw the ghost and ran away. That left my family." She gave a small smile and said, "I was excited to live here."

"You weren't scared?" Leo asked.

"No. Not at first," Tina Maria said. "I love my school. I love my friends. I love doing the math competition. And for a long time, we didn't see the ghost. My dad thought that maybe he went away."

That made Leo curious. "The General only had four kids. Who gets the house if you leave?"

"I don't know," Tina Maria said. "There's a distant cousin named José who told my mom he's not scared. He'd like to live here, but he's far away, learning how to make movies in college. We've never met." She added, "Mom says we should have the house torn down. No one wants to live in a haunted house."

"I don't think it has to be torn down," Michael said. "Let's find out more about this ghost." He set his Maker Sack on Tina Maria's desk and unzipped it. "Maybe your family will be the one who gets to stay!"

"I'd never live in a haunted house," Leo said, looking over the things Michael brought. "Never. Ever."

"You might not know it's haunted until you move in," Liv told him. "Ghosts are tricky like that."

"There's no such . . . ," Michael began, and all his friends chimed in, ". . . *thing as ghosts!*"

Michael laughed. "But if there was, here's how you can check." He admitted, "I learned a few things from Liv's *Suspicious Surprises* magazines."

"I didn't know you read my magazines!" Liv exclaimed happily.

"You leave them lying around the Maker Space," Michael said. "Sometimes I get bored. So I check them out." He gave Liv a grin. "We're gonna try out some ideas from the latest issue."

Michael pulled magnets, a flashlight, a thermometer, and a compass out of the Maker Sack.

He put the flashlight to the side. "We don't need this since it's still light out." He turned to Liv and asked, "Did you know the best ghost viewing hours are from nine at night to six in the morning?"

"Of course I knew that," Liv said. "And you should have brought red film to put over the light. The red light improves night vision."

"I didn't have any," Michael admitted. "Plus, it's still light out."

Leo wrinkled his nose. He said, "Did you know that ghosts will leave if you open a window? You also have to keep your shoes in the room. You're supposed to point the tips in different directions. It confuses them. It totally works. That's how I keep ghosts away at my house."

"That's silly," Michael snorted.

"We don't want to confuse the General's ghost," Liv said. "We want to talk to him."

"Let's try this," Michael said as he picked up his digital thermometer. When Michael pressed a button, the temperature in the room showed up on the screen.

"Ghosts bring the temperature of a room down," Liv explained to Tina Maria. "That's why people report feeling cold when there's a ghost around."

"When the General was here last night, I felt that!" Tina Maria said. "It was like a cold wind was blowing."

"I'm checking," Michael said. He looked at the display. "The temperature is steady. No ghost."

"The thermometer might be broken," Liv countered. "Check the compass."

She explained to the others, "If there's a ghost around, the compass dial will spin randomly because ghosts mess up the magnetic energy of the Earth."

Michael raised the small compass he'd bought at a garage sale. He stared at it for a long moment then said, "It's pointing north."

Liv and Leo leaned in to confirm.

"I think that's east," Leo said. "Or is it south?"

"Looks west to me," Liv said.

"*Hmm*," Michael said as he shook the compass. "It doesn't work."

"That's because the ghost is making it funky!" Liv said. She seemed very pleased with that answer.

Michael tossed the compass back in the Maker Sack.

He asked Tina Maria, "Do you have a needle, a cork, some scissors, and a cup of water?"

"Probably," Tina Maria said. "Why?"

"I'm going to make a new compass," Michael said. "Mine isn't working."

"Yes, it is!" Liv protested. "It's being spun by a ghostly spirit."

"I'll make a new one and try again," Michael repeated, ignoring Liv.

"It's still gonna spin," Liv assured Michael. "But you can try your best."

Tina Maria went to get the supplies Michael needed. When she returned, she said "Aunt Rosa just got here. She's packing up the room where the needles are kept. And Aunt Julia had to get a cork from a kitchen box. But I found everything you asked for."

She handed the supplies to Michael. "Thanks!" he said.

Michael picked up one of the magnets he'd brought along and rubbed the needle on it. "First I need to magnetize the needle," he explained. When he was done with the magnet, he set it aside.

Then, using Tina Maria's scissors, he cut a flat piece off the cork. He pushed the needle through the piece, then carefully placed it in the water. The cork and needle floated.

"The needle is pointing in just one direction," Leo announced. He looked out the window. The sun was slowly setting. "Sun sets in the west. So it's for sure pointing north."

"Right," Michael said, setting the homemade compass on Tina Maria's desk. "This proves it. No ghost."

"Whew," Leo said, wiping a hand across his forehead. "I feel so much better."

"It doesn't prove anything," Liv said. "So the spirit isn't in the room right this second. You already said that nine at night is a better haunting time. It's not even close to nine o'clock."

Michael declared, "There's no ghost."

Leo thought about it for a moment, then asked, "Michael, how do you explain that everyone who stays in the house sees a ghost? They hear a ghost? And that the ghost leaves threatening notes?"

"I think someone is trying to find the General's will," Michael said. "Once they find it, they can destroy the evidence and claim the house for themselves."

Tina Maria exclaimed, "It's impossible. Everyone's been scared away. No one wants this house."

"*Hmm.* That's true." Michael scratched his chin and said, "We need to find out more about your cousin, José. He's the most obvious suspect."

"José wants to live in this house and hasn't been scared away . . . yet," Leo said. "So maybe José made up a ghost and is scaring everyone else away. I *really* like the idea that there's no ghost."

"It's an interesting theory," Liv said. She put her hands on her hips and announced, "But it's totally wrong."

"Wrong?" Michael asked. "What makes you think I'm wrong?"

Liv pointed to the desk.

The compass in the cup was now spinning crazily. The needle was going round and round.

She hurried to the bed where Michael had put the thermometer.

"The temperature's dropped five degrees," Liv reported.

Tina Maria stared at Michael's ghost hunting props. She raised her fearful eyes, and announced, "The ghost is here."

CHAPTER SIX

It wasn't dark out yet, and still, it was spooky when the room lights flickered and then went completely off.

"Where's that flashlight?" Leo asked Michael. He was standing close to the bedroom door, ready to dash away.

"You don't need it," Michael said as the lights came back on. "But if it makes you feel better, here." He passed Leo the flashlight.

Leo immediately turned on the beam and swung it around the room. "Where are you, ghost?" he said in a whispered voice. "General Carlos, sir, don't hurt us."

"Oh, Leo," Liv said, marching into the center of the room. "Relax. We need to make contact." She raised her arms and said, "General Carlos, why are you here? How can we help you?"

Michael ignored Liv as she began chanting the General's name. "Pablo Carlos, Pablo Carlos . . ." She walked around the edges of the room, saying the name over and over again.

"Let me know if the ghost talks to her," Tina Maria said. "I want to check if Mom and Dad are back. They need to hear about this." She left to go find out.

"Leo," Michael said. "Do you still feel that cool breeze?"

"The one from the ghost?" Leo asked. "The one that made the temperature drop?"

"Yes," Michael said. He picked up the thermometer and looked at it. It was still cold in the room.

Leo took a moment to think about it and said, "Yes. It seemed to stop for a second, but I feel it again. It feels like a light wind."

"Let's find out where it's coming from," Michael said.

Liv had left her notebook on Tina Maria's bed. Michael told her, "Can I have a page of paper?"

Liv didn't answer. She had her eyes closed and was humming.

"I'll assume that means yes." Michael chuckled and shook his head.

While Liv channeled the ghost, Michael took the paper from her notebook and tore it into little strips. Then he went around the room, tossing up bits of paper like confetti.

Leo helped. "I don't know what we are doing, but it's fun!" he said as he joined in and threw some paper strips in the air by Tina Maria's desk.

"If the paper falls straight to the floor," Michael said, "then move to another place. We're looking for the wind to blow the paper."

"I found it!" Leo called out as he stood by the closet. When he tossed up the paper, the confetti blew back toward him. "The ghost is over here." Leo took two huge steps backward.

Michael came to inspect the area. He tossed more paper pieces in the air. "You're right. The confetti blows over here." He reached out to slide open the closet door.

"No. Don't." Leo tried to stop him. "The General might pop out!"

"There's no ghost," Michael said yet again. He opened the closet door. "See?"

Inside was a small, but powerful, fan. It was blowing cool air into the room through the slats in the closet door.

On a closer look, Michael discovered the fan was operated by a remote control. "Someone turned this on," he said. He reached forward and flicked the off switch.

Liv stopped chanting. "The fan might explain the chilly temperature, but what about the spinning compass?" she asked.

Michael thought about that. "Maybe I made it wrong? Or . . . a meteor might make it turn like that. Or maybe there's a mega-magnet in the room that is affecting it?"

Liv rolled her eyes. "There's no meteor. And no magnet. There's a ghost."

Michael had an idea. "Sometimes old houses like this have secret passages and hidden rooms. I wonder if that's how the person who left the fan is sneaking around."

"If only my computer worked," Leo moaned. "I could hack into the library's files and search for the architect's plans."

"Tina Maria has a computer. We could use it," Michael began, when suddenly Tina Maria shouted from downstairs.

"Michael, Liv, Leo — come quick!" Her voice echoed through the floorboards. "The General left another note!"

CHAPTER SEVEN

Liv and Michael ran down the steps with Leo right behind.

When they reached the living room, they found that everyone was there. Aunt Julia, Aunt Rosa, Uncle Federico, and Aunt Angelina. Even Tina Maria's parents.

They were all standing around a jar, just like the one that Tina Maria had brought to the Maker Shack.

Leo wondered if Michael would fingerprint everyone in the room. That's what Sheriff Kawasaki would do if she were there.

Tina Maria's mom was holding the note that had come inside it. "I found this in the upstairs closet," she reported. Then, she read it out loud: *"Leave my house. Be gone."*

"He's so bossy," Liv remarked. She turned to look at all the people in the room. "Okay, who got into a fight with the General when he was alive? Someone here made him mad."

No one confessed. No one seemed to think that the General was mad at them.

Michael asked Tina Maria's mom, "Can I see the note?"

While he studied it, Liv shouted to the air, "We come in peace!"

Leo inched his way toward the exit.

"Look!" Suddenly Aunt Rosa pointed at the large glass mirror. She said, "The General. He's here!"

Leo couldn't believe his eyes. The ghost in the mirror was exactly like Tina Maria had described. He looked identical to the painting in the hallway.

In fact, he was wearing the exact same military uniform with the exact same medals.

And just like Aunt Julia had said, he glowed with a dark brown shadow around his head and chest.

"Augh! That's an angry ghost," Leo shrieked. "I bet the compass is spinning like crazy!" They'd left all of Michael's ghost hunting tools up in Tina Maria's room. "We're doomed!"

The ghost didn't speak. There was a light hiss and a soft sputtering sound and then, the room fell completely silent.

Liv stepped closer to the mirror. She raised her arms high. "Welcome home, General Carlos. You'll find only friends here."

It was a nice greeting and for a moment, Leo thought that maybe Liv really did make some kind of contact. The image of the General shimmered for a second, faded out, then reappeared.

"He wants to talk to us!" Uncle Federico declared, pointing. "Look. He's moving his hand."

Sure enough, very slowly the General's hand was rising from the bottom of the mirror frame. He reached forward toward the people in the room.

"He is going to announce who he wants to live here," Liv declared as if she had heard him speak. She faced the ghostly image. "We can't find your will," Liv told the ghost. "Who should have the house?"

The ghost raised his finger and pointed.

"It's me," Rosa said. "I knew I should have never run away. He wasn't trying to scare me. Dad wanted to welcome me!"

"No, it's me," Federico said. "He knows that Angelina and I searched everywhere for the will. We have searched every book. We looked in every corner. Now, he is pointing to me. That means he wants us to come back!"

"No, wait," Aunt Julia said. "He's clearly pointing at me."

"I think he's pointing at Tina Maria's mom and dad," Leo said.

He added softly, "But maybe that's just because I want Tina Maria to stay here on Shaker Street."

"It's hard to tell," Liv said. "His finger keeps fading and coming back. It's too wiggly to see where he's pointing."

"He's pointing at me," a new voice said.

CHAPTER EIGHT

A man entered the room. He was young, tall, and had a mustache and short beard. The man was wearing a college sweatshirt.

"That's *gotta* be Cousin José," Michael whispered to Liv and Leo. "I wondered if he'd show up."

"Suspicious," Leo said, nodding.

It was like there was a puzzle in his head and pieces were starting to fit together.

José, the fan in Tina Maria's closet, the college sweatshirt, and that soft sound they'd heard when they first saw the General's ghost . . . But what did it all mean?! Leo's head hurt from thinking.

"I'm not afraid of ghosts," José declared loudly. He laughed, saying, "But I'm glad all of you are easily scared."

"I'm not scared," Federico said. "I —" He jumped as a huge shattering sound filled the room.

"Get back!" Tina Maria's dad leapt in front of his daughter and her friends. "I don't want you to get hurt."

The ghostly image in the mirror was gone. The mirror now lay in thousands of glass shards all over the living room floor.

There was a large piece by Michael's feet. He leaned down to touch it. "Ouch!" he quickly pulled back his hand.

"Did you get cut?" Leo asked.

"No," Michael said, showing Leo his hand. "I'm fine. But the glass is hot." He thought about that for a moment.

"It's hot?" Liv asked, reaching down to touch a piece herself.

"Careful," Tina Maria warned. Liv nodded as she pressed her hand against a large shard of the mirror glass.

"It is super hot!" Liv exclaimed. "Leo, want to touch it?"

"No thanks," he said. Leo stared at the pieces of mirror and watched as others in the room touched them. He asked Liv, "Can a ghost make something burning hot?"

She set the broken shard down on the floor and stepped away from it. "Ghosts are usually cool," she admitted. "Maybe the General is a special kind of poltergeist. I'd need to look it up."

"Too bad my computer's busted —" Leo started, then stopped. "Wait! That's it," he muttered. "This is just like my laptop."

"What are you talking about?" Liv asked.

Leo stood quietly thinking for a minute, then announced, "The ghost isn't a poltergeist." He wasn't so scared now, because he had a big idea about what was going on with the ghost in the mirror.

CHAPTER NINE

He looked to Michael. "The fan on my laptop makes a weird noise before it dies. Then, the whole thing gets too hot."

Michael smiled as he began to understand what Leo was thinking. "Go on," he prodded.

"A movie projector also uses a cooling fan to keep it from getting too hot," Leo said.

He looked over his shoulder at José. "I think José's using a projector to show a movie through the mirror. If I'm right, then his projector's fan is broken. When the projector gets too hot, everything around it gets hot too. The heat could have shattered the glass."

Leo moved toward the opening in the wall, but there was too much glass in the way.

"I think the projector is back there," he said. "We'll find it when we clean all this up."

"Impossible," Liv said. "It has to be a ghost. The General's finger moved!"

"Nah. That was José's finger," Leo said, feeling more and more confident that he had this mystery figured out.

"I don't know what you're talking about," José said.

"José is family. He would never do something like this," Aunt Rosa said.

"I know it sounds weird, but I spend a lot of time reading things online. I've read all about projecting videos through a mirror," Leo said.

He pointed to the broken mirror glass on the floor. "I'm pretty sure if you turn over a piece of the mirror," he continued, "you'll see the silver backing is scratched off. José had to do that to show the movie through the glass."

Sure enough, when Michael flipped over a piece of glass, the backing was rubbed off.

The family moved in to make a circle around José.

"Did *you* create the ghost?" Aunt Julia accused him. "Did *you* try to scare us all away?"

Before José answered, Michael realized what was going on.

"Are you learning how to make movies at college?" he cut in, as it all became clear.

"Well . . . ," José began.

"Yes, he is," Tina Maria said.

"Right! He's wearing a college sweatshirt," Leo said. "I knew that was an important clue!"

"You're all crazy," José said. "How can I be doing all this while I'm at school?"

Michael pointed at the sweatshirt. "That college isn't very far away. And if I took fingerprints, I bet it would prove that you've been playing tricks on your family."

"Well then, fingerprint him," Tina Maria's father said.

"Yes, fingerprint him," the others also said.

José looked around the room and sighed. "You don't have to. I'll confess. Look, I didn't mean any harm. It's true that I'm in film school. I'm working on my first movie. It's a horror film, and I wanted real-life emotions to make it authentic."

They all stared at him while he went on.

José explained, "I used to come here to visit the General when I was younger. We'd play hide and seek in the secret passages. When the old man died, I had this amazing idea for a movie. All I had to do was make up a story about a missing will and a haunted house!" He smiled and waved a hand at everyone, "You all were my actors."

"Does that mean you hid the will?" Tina Maria asked, eyes wide.

"Of course," José admitted. "That part was tricky. I used all my weekends and school holidays to make this film. The first time I came, I had to sneak in and take the will from the General's desk. Once I had it, I hid little cameras all over the house and waited to see what you all would do next." He pointed at Aunt Rosa. "It was lucky that she got scared so easily!"

Aunt Rosa frowned.

"I'd have told you all the truth eventually," José said. "I never really wanted to live here. I just said that to throw you off. I planned to give the General's will back at the movie's grand opening."

"But today, things went wrong. Your movie projector overheated," Michael said.

"Yeah, that was a bummer," José said.

"It was more than a bummer," said Aunt Julia. "It was dangerous."

José picked up a piece of broken glass. "You're right. I knew it had problems and was waiting for the new parts. That's why I haven't been here since Tina Maria's family moved in. But the parts never came, and I couldn't wait any longer. There's a big film festival coming up. I want to finish in time to enter my movie. My school's on semester break now," he said, "so here I am."

As everyone continued to glare at him, José went on, "When I snuck in last week, I brought an extra fan to cool the projector down. I discovered I could also use it to make ghost sounds. But today, I forgot the fan in Tina Maria's closet, and of course things got too hot."

"I'm calling the sheriff," Tina Maria's dad said. He pulled out his phone and started dialing. "You're in a lot of trouble."

"Stealing the will was illegal. So was breaking into the house to set things up," Leo told them all. "That's at least two crimes."

"Please don't call the sheriff," José pleaded. "I didn't mean any harm. I just wanted to get real reactions from people who honestly thought they were being haunted by a ghost."

"That's awful," Uncle Federico started.

"Not nice at all," Aunt Julia said.

"Hang on. I don't understand one thing." Federico asked, "Everyone else saw the ghost. But not me and Angelina. Why didn't we see it?"

"I was on a school trip that week," José admitted. "I couldn't get here and you moved out before the trip was over."

He pointed toward a tiny camera mounted on the ceiling. "My cameras were still running, though. Every normal creak in the house freaked you out. You should have seen your face when you hid in the closet. It was hysterical!"

"Grrr . . . ," Federico groaned angrily.

José pointed at Leo and said, "Uncle Federico was scared, but that kid will be the best one in the movie. He's going to be a star!"

"We'll never be as scared as Leo," Liv said with a laugh.

"Yeah," Leo agreed. "I'm a big chicken. But I also solved this mystery!"

"I'll be right back," Tina Maria told them. She hurried out of the living room and a minute later came back. She was carrying the General's portrait from the hallway. She held it up next to José.

"With a costume on, he'd look just like the General," Michael said.

"I made the ghost to be like a mini movie inside this bigger movie," José said. "I even added the brown shadow. I was very close to finishing when Tina Maria's friends showed up and ruined everything," José said, looking disappointed.

He shrugged before continuing. "Now I need a different ending. Everyone standing around and talking to me isn't scary. The ghost has to chase everyone away. When I'm done, this movie has to be scary!"

"You never fooled me," Liv said. "I knew it was a fake ghost."

Michael and Leo laughed.

"I'll put the painting back," Tina Maria said, and she started to walk out of the room.

"Hang on," Michael stopped her. "There's something on the back of the portrait. Can you turn the painting around?"

Tina Maria set the portrait of the General down. When she stepped aside, everyone could see there was an envelope taped to the back of the frame.

"It's the will!" Aunt Julia exclaimed.

"Yes," José said. "I put it there for safekeeping."

"Open it!" cried Uncle Federico. "We'll finally know who the house truly belongs to." He glared at José. "Tricking us just for a movie wasn't nice."

"I'm not upset. I'm going to be a movie star," Angelina said. She tossed back her hair like a celebrity.

"I'm going to be a star too," Aunt Rosa cheered.

Everyone stopped being mad that they'd been tricked. They started to get excited about being in a movie.

Tina Maria's father said, "So it seems I don't need to call the sheriff. Is everyone okay with that?"

Everyone nodded in agreement.

"What should we do with the will?" Tina Maria's mom asked.

"Since there's no real ghost, I think Rosa should get to keep the house. She's the oldest of us all. It's only fair," Aunt Julia said.

"I don't want it now," Aunt Rosa said. She smiled at Tina Maria. "I think Tina Maria should have the house. She's the General's only granddaughter. She loves her new school and is happy here. I say we let her have it."

"I agree," Leo said, thinking about the math competition.

Federico and Angelina liked the idea. "The house should be Tina Maria's," they said together.

Aunt Rosa came and kissed Tina Maria on the forehead. "You have to make us two promises. One, if you own this house, you'll let your mom and dad live here."

Tina Maria nodded and said, "Of course!"

"And," Aunt Rosa continued, "we all get to come visit any time we want!"

"It's a deal," Tina Maria agreed. "Thank you!" she said, going around the room to hug all her aunts and her uncle.

"But the will!" José begged them to open it. "You have to open it!"

He pointed up to the camera on the ceiling and said, "Reading it has to be part of the movie!"

"The will doesn't matter anymore," Uncle Federico said. "We've decided what's best for our family. I'm sure the General would have agreed with our choice." Uncle Federico asked his brothers and sisters for permission to destroy the document. "We can just say we never found it," he said, smiling.

When they all agreed, he took the envelope and tore it into confetti. He tossed the pieces up in the air. The scraps of paper came straight back down.

"Look! No wind," Leo said happily. "That means no more ghost."

CHAPTER TEN

Liv was busy typing on Leo's computer at Leo's desk in the Maker Shack. Michael had figured out the problem and fixed it when they got back from Tina Maria's house.

"What do you think Liv is up to?" Leo asked Michael as he put the digital thermometer back in a plastic bin. Michael set the bin on the shelf.

"I don't know," Michael replied. He called out, "Hey Liv, what are you doing?"

"I'm writing that article about General Carlos's ghost," Liv answered, not turning to them. "I told you that was my plan."

Liv was flipping through the notes in her journal. She'd read a little then go back to typing.

"I'm going to submit it to *Suspicious Surprises*," she explained.

Michael came over to stand behind her.

"Don't look!" Liv chased him away. "I'll show you when I'm ready."

"But there's a problem," he said. "The ghost was fake."

"You have no imagination," Liv said. She raised her head to look at Leo. "You don't either."

"Yes, I do," Leo countered.

"No, you don't," Liv told them both. "Just because José was pretending to be a ghost, it doesn't mean that the ghost of Pedro Carlos doesn't truly live in the old house."

"We proved he doesn't exist," Michael said. "Remember? Everything was explained."

Liv snorted. "Not everything. There was one thing left."

"What are you talking about?" Leo asked her. He felt the hairs on his neck rising.

"The compass was spinning all by itself. That means there really was a ghost in Tina Maria's room." Liv went back to writing.

Michael looked at Leo and shrugged. "I guess she could be right," he said. "Or it could have also been that there was a strong magnet in the room."

He held up his own magnet. "Magnets mess with compass directions," he added.

"That magnet is too weak to make a compass spin. Only an electromagnet could do what we saw," Liv said. "The compass proves it. The ghost of General Pedro Carlos now lives happily with Tina Maria and her family!"

YOU CAN BE A
MYSTERIOUS MAKER
TOO:

CURIOUS COMPASS

Things to find:

- Metal sewing needle
- Magnet (a refrigerator magnet will work)
- Cork
- Scissors
- Pliers
- Cup with water

What you do:

1. Rub the magnet on the needle at least five times. Always rub it in the same direction to magnetize it.
2. Cut a quarter-inch piece off the cork, like a small round circle.
3. Push the needle through the sides of the cork. You may need the pliers to pull it through. The length of needle should be even on each side of the cork.
4. Set the cork and needle into a cup filled with at least an inch of water.
5. Watch what happens! Which way is north?

FINGERPRINT FINDER

Things to find:

- Rubber or latex gloves
- Glass or metal object (these work best)
- Baby powder or a dark powder, such as ashes (use baby powder for dark colored objects and dark powder for light objects)
- Bowl
- Soft paintbrush or makeup brush

What you do:

1. Handle the glass or metal object carefully. Wear gloves to keep your own fingerprints off.
2. Pour a little powder in the bowl.
3. Dip brush into powder. Don't use too much.
4. Dust the powder lightly on glass or metal surface to reveal fingerprints!
5. If you want, you can use regular tape to lift off the fingerprints. Stick it on and peel it away to take the powder fingerprints along.

ABOUT THE AUTHOR

Stacia Deutsch is the author of more than two hundred children's books, including the eight-book, award-winning, chapter book series *Blast to the Past*. Her résumé also includes *Nancy Drew and the Clue Crew*, *The Boxcar Children*, and *Mean Ghouls*. Stacia has also written junior movie tie-in novels for summer blockbuster films, including *Batman, The Dark Knight* and *The New York Times* best sellers *Cloudy with a Chance of Meatballs Jr.* and *The Smurfs*. She earned her MFA from Western State where she currently teaches fiction writing.

ABOUT THE ILLUSTRATOR

Robin Boyden works as an illustrator, writer, and designer and is based in Bristol, England. He has first-class BA honors in illustration from the University of Falmouth and an MA in Art and Design from the University of Hertfordshire. He has worked with a number of clients in the editorial and publishing sectors including Bloomsbury Publishing, *The Phoenix* comic, BBC, *The Guardian*, *The Times*, Oxford University Press, and Usborne Publishing.

GLOSSARY

compass (KUHM-puhss)—an instrument with a magnetic pointer that always points north, used for finding directions

electromagnet (i-lek-troh-MAG-nit)—a magnet that is formed when electricity flows through a coil of wire

magnetic energy (mag-NET-ik EN-er-jee)—the energy within a magnetic field, resulting in various metals either repelling or attracting each other

magnetize (MAG-nuh-tize)—to make something magnetic, either by exposing it to an electric current or by attaching a magnet to it

meteor (MEE-tee-ur)—a piece of rock from space that falls to the earth

poltergeist (pohl-ter-gahyst)—a mischievous ghost thought to be the cause of mysterious noises, such as knocking

projector (pruh-JEK-tur)—a machine that shows slides or movies on a screen

will (WIL)—a legal document that contains instructions stating what should happen to someone's property and money when the person dies

TALK WITH YOUR FELLOW MAKERS!

1. Tina Maria thinks her house is haunted. Do you think she has good reasons to believe in ghosts? Explain and support your thoughts.

2. What did the Mysterious Makers of Shaker Street use or make to prove that the house was not haunted? How did each item prove or not prove the haunting?

3. Which other skills did the Mysterious Makers use to investigate the ghost? How did they use their senses and experience?

GRAB YOUR MAKER NOTEBOOK!

1. There is one mystery left unsolved at the end of the book. What is it? What would you do to solve that final mystery?

2. In which ways do the Mysterious Makers agree or disagree about the ghost? Write about a time when you disagreed with a friend and how you worked it out.

3. Try rewriting the scene where they find the second note from the General from Tina Maria's point of view. What are her thoughts and feelings?

THE FUN DOESN'T STOP HERE:

Discover more at www.capstonekids.com

- Videos & Contests
- Games & Puzzles
- Friends & Favorites
- Authors & Illustrators

Find cool websites and more books like this one at www.facthound.com. Just type in the Book ID: 9781496546784 and you're ready to go!

READ MORE MAKERS ADVENTURES!

JF
DEU

10171337

Deutsch, Stacia,
That's the spirit!